MOPSY
THE WONDER DOG

by Marion Veal

The Atkinson Hyperlegible font used in this book has been specifically developed by Applied Design Works for low vision and visually impaired readers.
It is named after J. Robert Atkinson,
the founder of the Braille Institute of America.

First published in the UK in 2022

Text copyright © 2022 Marion Veal
Illustrations © 2022 Shanée Buxton
Photo © 2022 Mark Maton

ISBN: 978-1-7396329-5-3

Dedicated to Mopsy,
our brave little MopStar,
and all her Murmurator friends.

Mopsy was a little dog

And Mopsy loved to dream.

Sometimes she was a pirate,

Sometimes she was a queen.

Sometimes she was a pilot

Soaring through the sky,

But in all the dreams that Mopsy had,

She only had one eye.

The only eye that Mopsy had

Worked just as good as two,

And Mopsy wore an eyepatch

Sometimes pink and Sometimes blue.

Mopsy used her super nose

To hunt for buried treasure.

Mopsy used her ears to hear

The bees buzz in the heather.

Mopsy dreamed that she would be

An explorer in the park,

Mopsy drove a racing car,

It was really just a box.

She had a favourite Teddy

That was made from some old socks.

Mopsy liked to meet her friends

Robin, Fox and Mouse.

She had to crouch down very low

To see Hoggy in her house.

Mopsy had a party

And invited quite a crowd.

Her birthday cake was very tall

The top was in a cloud.

Mopsy only had one eye

But Mopsy loved to dream.

And Mopsy's favourite thing of all

Was chicken stew ice cream.

Caring For A One-Eyed Dog

Dogs can live long, happy lives with only one eye.

They will need time to adapt and learn how to do things differently.

Talk to them as you approach them so as not to startle them.

You may need to look out for obstacles on their 'blind side', as they may not see them.

Give your dog more time to sniff while on walks; it will help them learn about their environment.

Remember you may be more worried about your dog's changed appearance than they are.

People With Sight In Only One Eye

People will also adjust to being able to see out of only one eye.

Just like Mopsy your brain needs time to adapt to doing things differently.

You may need to move the book you are reading instead of your eye.

You may find it harder to judge depth and distances, for example when going up or down stairs.

But you will soon get the hang of things.

Mopsy's Story

The real Mopsy is a rescue dog from Greece.

She lived at The Greek Animal Rescue before finding her forever home in England.

Mopsy developed glaucoma and lost the sight in her left eye. Eventually she had to have the eye removed.

It was a difficult time but since her operation Mopsy has recovered well, and is a very happy dog once more.

Marion Veal
Author

Marion has always loved and cared for animals.

She is a science teacher and wildlife enthusiast.

Marion shares her home with two cats, her garden with a variety of wildlife and loves meeting Mopsy, and her human friends, for long walks by the sea.

Shanée Buxton
Illustrator

Shanée is passionate about art and wildlife. Illustrating Marion's books brings these passions together.

Marion and Mopsy

A proportion of the profits from this book will be donated to The Greek Animal Rescue.

Other books by Marion Veal

Vix, the Lockdown Fox

Mew, the Rescue Cat

Henry's New Home (Tales from The Rock Pool)

Harriet's Visit (Tales from the RockPool)

Website: marionveal.com

Printed in Great Britain
by Amazon

85991433R00018

Mopsy only has one eye but that does not stop her having lots of adventures and dreaming of more.

ISBN 978-1-7396329-5-3

9 781739 632953 >

BOOK ONE

Meditation for Children

Guided Imagery to Release Anxiety and Worries

WRITTEN BY IRIT ALMOG
ILLUSTRATED BY ALINE HEISER